Teamwork/\

WORM and Farmer Maguire

by Jeff Dinardo

illustrated by John Joven

RED
CHAIR
•PRESS•

Please visit our website at **www.redchairpress.com**.
Find a free catalog of all our high-quality products for young readers.

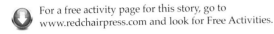

For a free activity page for this story, go to
www.redchairpress.com and look for Free Activities.

Worm and Farmer Maguire: Teamwork/Working Together

Publisher's Cataloging-In-Publication Data
(Prepared by The Donohue Group, Inc.)

Dinardo, Jeffrey.
Worm and Farmer Maguire : teamwork/working together / by Jeff Dinardo ; illustrated by
John Joven.
p. : col. ill. ; cm. -- (Funny bone readers)
Summary: Farmer Maguire loves his garden. Worm loves to work in her garden home. Can
the two learn to work together? This illustrated story shows young readers that everyone's
contribution to a task is important. Book features: Big Words and Big Questions.
Interest age level: 004-006.
ISBN: 978-1-939656-19-3 (lib. binding/hardcover)
ISBN: 978-1-939656-07-0 (pbk.)
ISBN: 978-1-939656-26-1 (ebook)
1. Cooperativeness--Juvenile fiction. 2. Gardens--Juvenile fiction. 3. Worms--Juvenile fiction.
4. Farmers--Juvenile fiction. 5. Cooperativeness--Fiction. 6. Gardens--Fiction. 7. Worms--
Fiction. 8. Farmers--Fiction. I. Joven, John. II. Title.
PZ7.D6115 Wo 2014

[E]   2013937171

This series first published by:
Red Chair Press LLC   PO Box 333   South Egremont, MA 01258-0333

Printed in the United States of America

1 2 3 4 5 18 17 16 15 14

Farmer Maguire had a beautiful garden.
It was filled with neat rows of vegetables.

Every day Farmer Maguire worked in his garden. He pulled the weeds. He watered the plants, and he cared for plants that were sick.

All his neighbors said it was
a wonderful garden.

Just beneath the plants lived Worm.
She also loved to work in the garden.

Every night she tunneled under the plants. She made the soil soft so the roots could grow.

She chewed the weeds she found. All her friends said it was a wonderful garden.

One morning Worm could not sleep.
She made her way to the surface.
She saw Farmer Maguire at work.

Farmer Maguire tilled the soil.
He harvested tomatoes and he
planted a new row of carrots.

"So he works in the garden too," Worm thought. "And he does much more work than me."

Worm slowly crawled back home.
"The garden would do fine without me,"
she sighed.

That night Worm did not work in the garden. She crawled up onto a tomato and stared at the moon. Just before dawn, she fell asleep.

That morning, Worm woke with a
start. She was still on the tomato
and someone was picking her up.
It was Farmer Maguire.

"You are the farmer,"
said Worm sadly.
"I used to work here, too."

Farmer Maguire laughed.
"So *you* must be the one who
has been helping me," he said.

"I don't do much," said Worm.
"You do most of the work. You till
the soil and you water the plants."

"The garden would not grow well without you," said the farmer. "You help the roots grow and keep the plants healthy."

Farmer Maguire and Worm spent
the rest of the morning talking.

They talked about the best month to plant
beans and which vegetables were their
favorites.

The farmer gently placed Worm back
on the ground.
"Your garden is the nicest one around,"
said Worm.

"You mean *our* garden," said Farmer Maguire. Worm smiled as she crawled back home.

Worm knew she had a busy
night's work ahead of her.

Big Questions: Farmer Maguire loved his garden. What did Worm do to help in the garden? Why do you think Farmer Maguire was happy Worm helped out?

Big Words:

harvested: gathered crops when they are ready to eat or use

till: make land ready to plant crops in the ground

vegetables: plants that are usually green, red, or orange eaten as food